Hold on to Your Hat, Noddy

INDEX

It was a wild and windy day in Toy Town…

The wind blew a piece of paper along and – SLAP – it landed right on the windscreen of Noddy's car.

"What a windy day!" said Noddy, setting off for Toadstool House to see his friend, Big-Ears.

"Are you ready, Big-Ears?" Noddy called,
as he parked his car. "It's a great day for fishing!"
    But Big-Ears was inside his house, peering
up the chimney.
    "There's a change of plan, Noddy," he said.
    "Oh no!" cried Noddy. "What's happened?"

Big-Ears shook his head. "I'm afraid it's much
too windy to go out on the lake."

"Oh, dear," said Noddy, sadly. "Can we play
ball in the garden instead?"

"Sorry, Noddy," replied Big-Ears. "We can't
go outdoors at all today."

"We can play *indoors* then," said Noddy, cheerfully.

"We can't do that either," said Big-Ears. "It's very cold in here and I can't light the fire because there's an old bird's nest blocking my chimney."

"No problem," replied Noddy. "I'll climb up on to the roof and clear it out for you, Big-Ears."

"I can't let you go up the ladder in this wind, it's too dangerous," said Big-Ears, as he peered up the chimney. "The weather just won't let us enjoy ourselves today."

"Oh, what a gloomy day," grumbled Noddy.

But he wasn't going to let the wild weather get the better of him.

"I'll find a way to cheer you up, Big-Ears," he called as he rushed out.

Big-Ears looked up. "Thank you, Noddy, but I'm not gloomy…"

An avalanche of soot whooshed into the room.

"Ahhhhhhh-choooo!" sneezed Big-Ears.

Out in the street, Tessie Bear was struggling to keep hold of her knitting bag. The wind had blown it up like a balloon and it was pulling her along.

"What a wind!" she squealed. Noddy jumped out of his car to help.

"Would you like a ride home, Tessie?"

But riding in Noddy's car was even breezier.

"Ohhh! This wind wants to steal my hat!"
said Tessie Bear, using one of her knitting needles
as a hat pin. "What a gloomy day!"

"Yes," Noddy agreed. "It's made Big-Ears
gloomy. I wish I could cheer him up."

Tessie Bear thought for a moment.

"How about… a party?"

"Brilliant!" cried Noddy. "I know, let's have a *surprise* party. We can invite everyone to Big-Ears' house."

"Shouldn't we tell him first?" asked Tessie Bear.

"It wouldn't be a surprise, then," said Noddy.

The wind blew more and more wildly as Noddy
and Tessie Bear walked through Toy Town inviting
their friends to Big-Ears' party.

"Now *we'd* better go to the party," said Tessie.

"Mrs Skittle is taking a cake, Mr Plod has a party game and Mr Sparks is bringing a heater!" Noddy told Tessie Bear.

"What shall *we* take, Noddy?" asked Tessie Bear.

"Balloons!" whooped Noddy, gleefully.

Noddy and Tessie Bear drove to Dinah Doll's stall.
"Don't close your stall yet, Dinah!" called Noddy.
"It's too windy to stay open, Noddy," said Dinah.
"But we need big balloons for Big-Ears' surprise
party!" Noddy explained.

"I can't say no to that!" said Dinah, and she gave Noddy a handful of balloons.

"Thanks, Dinah," said Noddy. "See you at the party."

"You'd better get indoors quickly," said Dinah. "It's just too windy!"

As Dinah shut up her stall,
Noddy and Tessie Bear set off in Noddy's car
for Big-Ears' house. Suddenly, the car coughed
and spluttered… and stopped!

"What's wrong?" cried Tessie Bear.

"We're out of petrol," said Noddy.
"And we're going to miss Big-Ears' party!"

But Tessie Bear had an idea.

"Let's blow up the balloons and tie them to the car. Then the wind will pull us along like a sailing boat."

Soon the car was covered with brightly coloured balloons. Tessie Bear's idea worked! The harder the wind blew, the faster the car sailed along, its wheels hardly touching the ground.

"This is fun!" Noddy shouted.

Soon the car was zooming along faster and faster.
"Oh, no!" Noddy cried. "We're going *too* fast!"
"Put the brake on, Noddy!" yelled Tessie Bear.
Noddy jammed his foot down on the brake,
but it was too late. The car had started to lift off
the ground!

Then… WHOOSH!
   The wild wind swept the car up
into the sky.
   "H-E-L-P!" yelled Noddy and Tessie Bear.

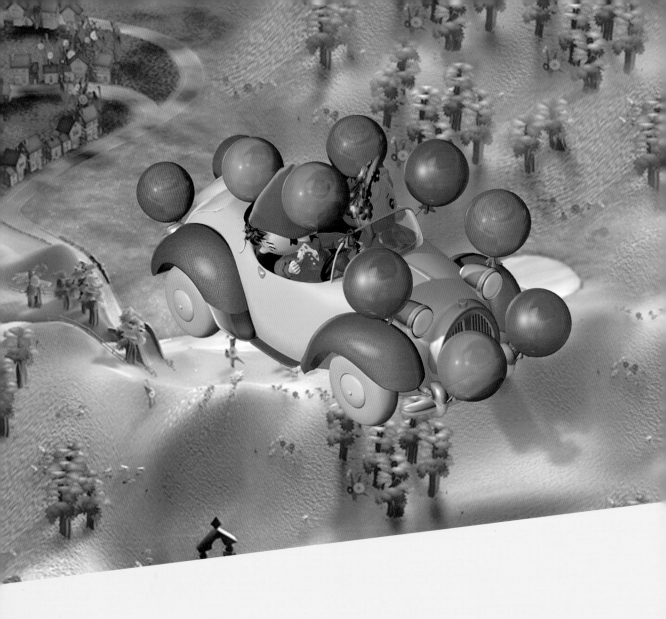

Terrified, Noddy and Tessie Bear peered over the side of the car. As they rose higher and higher, Toy Town looked smaller and smaller.

"What can we do, Noddy?" cried Tessie Bear.

Meanwhile, at Big-Ears' house, the party was in full swing. They had played Mr Plod's game and started on the cakes. There was so much jolly chatter and laughter, Big-Ears almost didn't hear Dinah Doll knocking at the door.

"Cheer up, Big-Ears!" said Dinah Doll, as he opened the door.

"Why does everyone think I need cheering up?" said Big-Ears.

"Noddy told us you were gloomy," Dinah Doll told him.

"But I'm not!" chuckled Big-Ears.

"And speaking of Noddy, where is he?"

Noddy and Tessie Bear were clinging on for dear life. The wind was blowing harder than ever.

"STOP IT, WIND!" shouted Noddy. "Put us down or… I'll tell Big-Ears!"

"I don't think the wind is listening," said a very scared Tessie Bear.

The car lurched to one side and the knitting needle
holding Tessie's hat on poked into Noddy.

"I know!" said Noddy. "Let's use your knitting
needle to burst the balloons and get back down!"

"Good idea," agreed Tessie Bear.

POP! POP! POP! Tessie popped three balloons and the car began to drop.

"Look, Tessie! The wind is taking us right down to Big-Ears' doorstep!" Noddy shouted.

Back in Toadstool House, Big-Ears knelt down
in front of his fireplace.

"I wish I could light a fire," he muttered.
"And where can Noddy and Tessie Bear be?"

THUMP! Something big clunked on
to the roof. What was that?

Everyone ran outside to have a look.

It was Tessie Bear and Noddy – on the roof
of Big-Ears' house!

"What a terrible piece of parking!" said
Mr Plod and everyone laughed.

Noddy reached into the chimney and pulled
out an old bird's nest. "Now you can have a nice
cosy fire, Big-Ears!" he shouted.

"Thank you, Noddy, for clearing my chimney,"
said Big-Ears, "in all that wind!"

"What a gloomy day," sighed Noddy.

"No, Noddy," smiled Big-Ears. "With friends
like you, every day is a good day!"

This edition published 2004 for Index Books Limited

First published in Great Britain by HarperCollins Publishers Ltd in 2002

1 3 5 7 9 10 8 6 4 2

ISBN: 0 00 770122 5

Printed and bound in China